Full Moon Night in Silk Cotton Tree Villa

A Collection of Caribbean Folk Tales

Written by John Agard and Grace Nichols

Illustrated by Rosie Woods

Contents

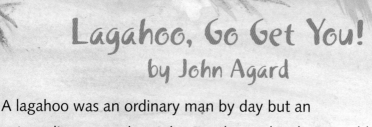

Lagahoo, Go Get You!
by John Agard

A lagahoo was an ordinary man by day but an extraordinary man by night. For then, a lagahoo would change himself into a wolf and go around eating humankind, even little humankind, namely children.

But had anyone from Silk Cotton Tree village actually seen a lagahoo? After all, that's how Silk Cotton Tree village got its name in the first place. People were always seeing things.

It all started with that silk cotton tree that grew in the middle of the village. Two French engineers were about to cut it down in order to build a road. But after one strike from their axes, they both dropped dead on the spot.

They'd taken no notice of the islanders' warning that the silk cotton tree was the home of ghosts, duppies and jumbies – call them whatever you please.

Hurt and angry with humankind for daring to chop it, the silk cotton tree released some spookies, including Lagahoo, the wolf man, to haunt the island.

But could it be true that your own grandpapa was a lagahoo?

3

This was a question Lil Piece wanted to ask his grandpapa, who was the shoemaker of Silk Cotton Tree island. Lil Piece wasn't his real name but his nickname, for he was very small for his age.

Of course, Lil Piece couldn't very well come right out and say, "Grandpapa, is true you're a lagahoo?" So Lil Piece introduced the subject gently. "Grandpapa, I read in a big book at school how lagahoo comes from loup garou, the French word for werewolf ... "

"Boy, mind all dat reading 'bout the werewolf don't turn you into a lagahoo," was all Grandpapa said before carrying on with his work.

"Boy, what wrong? Why you looking at me like dat?"

Then Lil Piece came out with what was really troubling his mind. "Grandpapa, Bully-Boy at school say how you is shoemaker by day and lagahoo by night. Is true?"

Instead of looking shocked or upset, Grandpapa burst into one big belly laugh. "Me? Lagahoo? Well, boy, today you sweeten me with a sweet-sweet joke! How did Bully-Boy come up with a tale like dat?"

Lil Piece said that Bully-Boy's father was the village milkman. He'd never forgiven Lil Piece's grandpapa for accusing him of diluting his customers' milk with water.

"I shoulda guessed," Lil Piece's grandpapa said. "I shoulda guessed dat nobody but Bully-Boy's daddy would spread a rumour like dat. So I is a lagahoo? Very well, if I is a lagahoo, I is a lagahoo."

When his grandpapa explained what he had in mind, Lil Piece could only smile at his grandpapa's love of playing pranks.

It would be their little secret. Nobody, not even Lil Piece's mother and father, must know that Grandpapa was about to make a pair of wolf heads. One for himself; one for his grandson.

Since Grandpapa had designed many carnival costumes (three times in a row he'd won the Silk Cotton Tree Mask-Man trophy), he soon knocked together a pair of wolf heads. He used the trimmed white of yuca for long scary fangs and two cherry-bright cricket balls for staring eyes.

"Lagahoo Senior and Lagahoo Junior," Lil Piece laughed.

That very night, outside the gate of Bully-Boy's big white house, Lil Piece and his grandpapa gave the performance of their lives. It was so spine-chilling, the moon herself couldn't ask for a better pair of howlers.

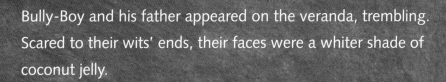

Bully-Boy and his father appeared on the veranda, trembling. Scared to their wits' ends, their faces were a whiter shade of coconut jelly.

"Lagahoo!" the milkman screamed.

He promptly rushed back inside, double-locked the front door, and the same with the bedroom door.

Meanwhile, back at Grandpapa's workshop, Lil Piece was in stitches. "Nice one, Grandpapa, nice one."

The following day, when Grandpapa asked the milkman, "How life treating you?" the milkman admitted that he hadn't slept a wink all night because of a visit from a lagahoo.

"Two lagahoo in fact. A big-man lagahoo and a half-size lagahoo. Now my poor son stares into space, mumbling, 'lagahoo lagahoo' to heself."

Grandpapa had to nudge Lil Piece who couldn't keep his giggles down.

"Don't you worry," said Grandpapa to the milkman.

Then Grandpapa, just for a laugh, advised the milkman to take his pointer broom, made from the spines of palm leaf – the very same broom that he used to sweep up the fowl dung from the front of his yard. "Make sure you sleep with that broom near your pillow," he said. "One smell, and quick-time, the lagahoo will rush back to rest in the silk cotton tree."

The milkman thanked Grandpapa for the advice and even apologised for spreading the rumour that Grandpapa was himself a lagahoo.

"Let bygones be bygones," Grandpapa said, as they shook hands.

But truth, they say, is stranger than fiction. That weekend, the village's newspaper had a headline splashed big and bold:

ONE OF THE MILKMAN'S COWS FOUND DEAD! LAGAHOO SUSPECTED!

According to the newspaper, the police were puzzled that some blood taken from the scene of the crime had revealed traces of both human and wolf. They asked people who'd seen the lagahoo to come forward.

When Lil Piece had finished reading the article, Grandpapa couldn't believe his ears. Perhaps lagahoo were real after all! He turned to Lil Piece and said, "Now you see why we does always warn all you children: Lagahoo, go get you!"

The Candlefly and the Hunters
by Grace Nichols

One day, in a forest village, a group of men were playing cards.
They sat around a table in a benab, a kind of thatched round house.
They were having a good time, when one of the men noticed a tiny
fly on the edge of the table. He was just about to bring his heavy
hand down on it when another said kindly, "Oh leave the little
creature; it isn't harming anyone."

And so the fly was spared. To everyone's amazement, the tiny creature turned to the kind man and said, "Oh thank you, sir, for saving my life. Some day I hope to repay you for your kind deed."

The others laughed at the idea that a tiny fly could help anyone, and slapped their thighs in amusement.

A few days later, the men set out hunting with their bows and arrows, in search of some wild meat for their families to eat.

This meant crossing the river to the other side, where creatures like the iguana and the chachalaka bird could be found.

Their small boat took them over to the other side of the forest.
Everyone was in good spirits as they walked through
the thick bushes, and they sang an old folk song:

> *Mosquito says I will zwing O,*
> *Mosquito says I will zwing O,*
> *Zwing O, Zwing O.*

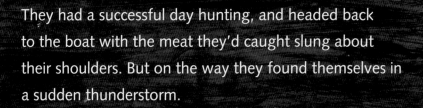

They had a successful day hunting, and headed back
to the boat with the meat they'd caught slung about
their shoulders. But on the way they found themselves in
a sudden thunderstorm.

They couldn't seek shelter under the trees because, of course,
lightning can split a tree in two with one zigzagging flash.

So they stood there huddled together in the open.
They jumped at every crackle, thinking it might be
a jaguar or an anaconda snake.

Eventually, the blinding rain stopped, but it was already night. The men could barely see as they made their way back to the boat on the river.

They paddled quickly in the dark, but when they came to a fork in the river they couldn't see which way to take. There was no moon, not even a single star to help them. Soon they were hopelessly lost.

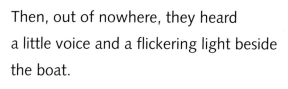

Then, out of nowhere, they heard
a little voice and a flickering light beside
the boat.

"Can I be of any help?" the voice said.
"I'm the little candlefly whose life you spared."

The hunters couldn't believe their eyes or ears.
They had a saviour! One in the shape of
a candlefly.

The man who had almost squashed the fly felt ashamed. "Forgive me," he said, "for being so thoughtless. We're lost and can't find our way home in the dark."

"Just follow me," said the candlefly. "I'm glad to repay the kindness of the gentleman here who told you not to kill me."

So they followed the flickering candlefly down the dark river, through the sleeping forest. Their candlefly guide flew on and on, taking them safely to their benab homes.

Their families were so happy to have them back that they wanted to do something in return for the candlefly.

The kind hunter's little daughter had an idea. "Father, why don't we have a candlefly dance every month for our candlefly friends?"

And so it was done.

The next day, as evening fell, everyone gathered in
a forest clearing. They laid out special dishes and drinks.
The children were all dressed up in shimmering capes
and could hardly wait for the celebrations to begin.

The candleflies arrived, like magical little aliens,
and the village flute players began to play their music.

At that moment, the boys and girls started swaying and twirling.
The candleflies danced around them, delighted.

And to this day, every month in that forest village,
the candlefly dance shimmers on.

Meet Mama Water
by John Agard

In her seagrass blouse, shell earrings and crown of gleaming coral, Mama Water was beautiful. She watched over rivers, lakes and swamps like they were her children. She called sea creatures "her precious darlings".

But be warned, from her waist down, Mama Water was in fact all snake. A nine metre, full-bellied, green anaconda.

Of course, Mama Water always made sure her anaconda bottom half was well hidden under water, only revealing her stunning top half to others.

One night, she was sitting on a rock in her favourite lagoon, braiding her hair, when she spotted a young fisherman. He was a kindly man who always returned the little fish to the sea. He caught only enough to feed himself, his mother and a little extra for a neighbour or a hungry stranger passing through Silk Cotton Tree village.

On this particular night, he was scattering flowers from his boat to the river. This was his way of saying thanks to the river for providing the fish that kept him alive.

"How sweet," thought Mama Water. Then she shook her head and said, "Get a grip of yourself, Mama Water. Don't go all softie-softie. He just another human. And humans pollute rivers. I'll teach him a lesson."

There and then, she made one thunderous splash. The sudden commotion sent the fisherman flying out of his boat, into the water. And although he was a fisherman, he didn't know how to swim.

But Mama Water took him in her arms, and her swirling embrace put him under her spell. He felt safe and snug, as if in a dream.

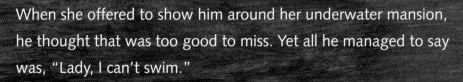

When she offered to show him around her underwater mansion, he thought that was too good to miss. Yet all he managed to say was, "Lady, I can't swim."

Before you could say "flying fish", Mama Water had taught him the backstroke, the breaststroke, the tortoise flip and the porpoise dip.

The fisherman couldn't believe he was actually swimming amongst shrimps that glowed and dolphins that spun like ballet dancers. Around him, all sorts of strange plants and rocks flickered with light. He was so happy here, he agreed to live with Mama Water in her lagoon mansion for six months and a day.

But after a while, he began missing little things about Silk Cotton Tree village. The new-morning crowing of a cockerel. The no-nonsense braying of a donkey. The Sundays he spent playing beach cricket. And of course his mother in the hammock telling him old-time stories.

It made Mama Water sad to see him so sad, missing his earth home as much as he did.

So she agreed to let him return home as long as he promised to come back after six months and a day.

But even as he was waving goodbye, the fisherman began to think she must be the Mama Water his mother had warned him about. The one who'd led many men down to a watery grave. While he was in her mansion he'd been under her spell, but now he was free he knew the truth.

Back on dry land, the first thing the fisherman did was take off his left shoe. Then he headed for home, walking backwards. Yes, he walked all the way backwards without his left shoe. Exactly as his mother had told him to do, if he ever needed to escape the spell of Mama Water.

And of course, when six months and a day had come to pass, Mama Water waited there on that rock, braiding her hair in the full moon.

That same night, the fisherman turned to his mother. "Full moon tonight, Ma," he said, as if in a dream. "I think I'll go take a swim."

His mother looked up. "Boy, since when could you swim?"

But the fisherman didn't reply – he just smiled, still spellbound after all, as he sleepwalked towards Mama Water's favourite lagoon.

Moongazer and Fearless Freddie
by Grace Nichols

Beware, beware,
when the moon is bright,
Moongazer-monster
rules the night.

Moongazer was said to be
a tall-tall man, even taller than
a lamppost. On full-moon night he
would appear with his legs open
across the path you needed to take.

He never looked down to earth but
just stared up at the moon. Yet he
could sense if anyone walked
between his legs. If anyone dared
to pass, this Moongazer would
close his legs with a snap and
the poor person would be crushed
as flat as a pancake.

This made all the children stay indoors in their beds on full-moon night with their curtains pulled tight. They were terrified in case Moongazer decided to take a walk and peep in at their bedroom window.

All except for one little boy whose nickname was "Fearless Freddie" who didn't seem scared of anything.

Freddie's parents often told him off because he didn't listen to them. But then he always gave them such a sweet smile that their anger would melt away like the morning mist.

Well, Fearless Freddie had already decided to see for himself if this story about Moongazer was really true. He could hardly wait for the next full-moon night to come.

And come it did, a beautiful big full moon.

Fearless Freddie kissed his parents goodnight with his sweet smile and went up to his room. Soon he was climbing through his bedroom window and hopping onto the branches of the nearby mango tree which almost touched the house. Very quietly he made his way down.

No one was on the road at that hour, just Freddie and
the moonlight. On and on he walked but he could see
nothing that looked like a moongazer.

Then he came to a narrow tree-lined lane. Freddie noticed
a sign on a tree at the entrance. It said quite simply:

BEWARE, MOONGAZER MAN
HAS BEEN SEEN IN THIS AREA.

Anyone else would have turned around and started running for
their life, but not our boy, Freddie. He walked fearlessly down
the lane but saw nothing except for
the swaying spooky trees.

"Just as I did think, a lot of
jumbie nonsense to scare us,"
he murmured. When he got to
the end of the lane, he turned back
and began to make his way home.

But then he saw a sight that made
his blood run cold.

Standing before him, was
the figure of a tall-tall man
blocking his path.

Fearless Freddie blinked, then blinked again. Yes, it was none other than Moongazer – legs open, gazing up at the moon!

He could hear his heart thumping. Budoops-Budoops-Budoops. Frozen with fright, he thought, "Should I make a dash for it between the creature's legs? Or should I hide out behind the spooky trees until morning?"

He didn't want to do either, but he made a sudden Fearless-Freddie decision. He was a good runner so he dashed, but Moongazer's legs came together in a flash.

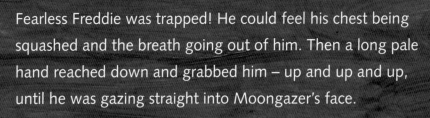

Fearless Freddie was trapped! He could feel his chest being squashed and the breath going out of him. Then a long pale hand reached down and grabbed him – up and up and up, until he was gazing straight into Moongazer's face.

Well, the sight of Moongazer's eyes scared the life out of Freddie. His eyes were like two huge torch lights, cold and deadly.

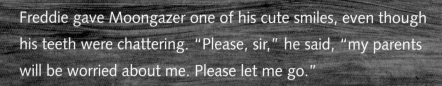

Freddie gave Moongazer one of his cute smiles, even though his teeth were chattering. "Please, sir," he said, "my parents will be worried about me. Please let me go."

To hear a Moongazer laugh was something else. Perhaps he'd never laughed before in his life. His laughter reached deep into the leaves and roots of the trees.

"*Please, sir, please, sir.*" Moongazer copied Freddie's cries. The voice chilled Freddie to the bone.

Moongazer began to stride away with Freddie who kicked
and squirmed. How could he escape from Moongazer?

"I'm not afraid of you," Freddie lied.

This made Moongazer stop in his tracks. His eyes rolled in
his head and he looked more terrible than ever. "Not afraid
of me! We'll see about that!" Then he stared again at Freddie.
Stared hard into his eyes.

"Wait – you're a moonshine baby! I can tell from the spark
in your eyes!"

43

Freddie nodded quickly. His mother had once told him that he was born on a full-moon night. But what did that mean? He soon found out.

"I don't touch moonshine babies!" Moongazer bellowed, and he tossed poor Freddie away as fast as he could.

To Freddie, it seemed as if he was falling forever, then he hit some water with a great splash. Yes, he landed in a river. Lucky, lucky Freddie.

It was one tired, wet little boy who made his way home that morning just as the sky was beginning to lighten. He managed somehow to make it back up the mango tree and into his bedroom.

And there we must leave him, Fearless Freddie, who's not so fearless now, for he's seen eyes no earthly child should ever see.

The magic of Silk Cotton
Tree village

47

Ideas for reading

Written by Clare Dowdall, PhD
Lecturer and Primary Literacy Consultant

Reading objectives:
- identify themes and conventions
- discuss words and phrases that capture the reader's interest and imagination
- discuss their understanding and explain the meaning of words in context

Spoken language objectives:
- participate in discussions, presentations, performances, role play, improvisations and debates

Curriculum links: Geography – locational knowledge

Resources: atlas or maps; ICT for research

Build a context for reading

- Read the title. Ask children what they know about the full moon, and what special things legends say happen at full moon.
- Look at the front cover and read the title. Find the Caribbean on a map and discuss what it might be like there.
- Read the blurb. Ask children what a lagahoo and candlefly might be, based on the cover illustrations.

Understand and apply reading strategies

- Read pp2–3 together, and discuss whether lagahoos (werewolves) appear in any other stories they know.
- Ask children to describe what happened in Silk Cotton Tree village to make it a special place.
- Look at the question at the end of p3. Ask children to think about how this affects them as a reader.
- Ask children to continue reading to find out whether Lil Piece's Grandpapa is a lagahoo, and what happens in the other stories.